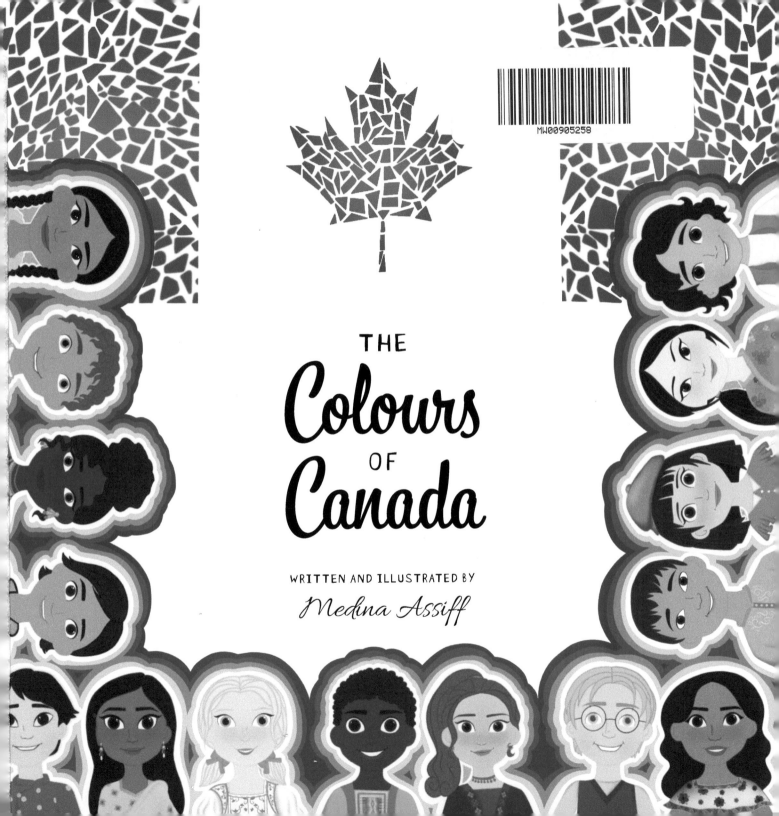

THE
Colours
OF
Canada

WRITTEN AND ILLUSTRATED BY

Medina Assiff

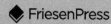 FriesenPress

One Printers Way
Altona, MB R0G 0B0
Canada

www.friesenpress.com

ISBN
978-1-03-911776-1 (Hardcover)
978-1-03-911775-4 (Paperback)
978-1-03-911777-8 (eBook)

1. JUVENILE FICTION, PEOPLE & PLACES, CANADA

Distributed to the trade by The Ingram Book Company

For Aleena

On the first day of school, Miss Onya pulls out a box labeled, "The Colours of Canada." The box is filled with lots of pretty coloured tiles. Miss Onya gives each student in her class a different colour.

"Today," Miss Onya joyfully says, "we will be making a mosaic of Canada."

The Colours of Canada

Beniko asks, "What's a mosaic, Miss Onya?"

"A mosaic," answers the teacher, "is a bunch of different coloured tiles working together to make a single picture."

"How will we make one of Canada using only one colour?" Mariano questions.

"We will all work together, Mariano," explains Miss Onya. "If we want to show Canada's true beauty, all of your unique cultural backgrounds and tiles must be included!"

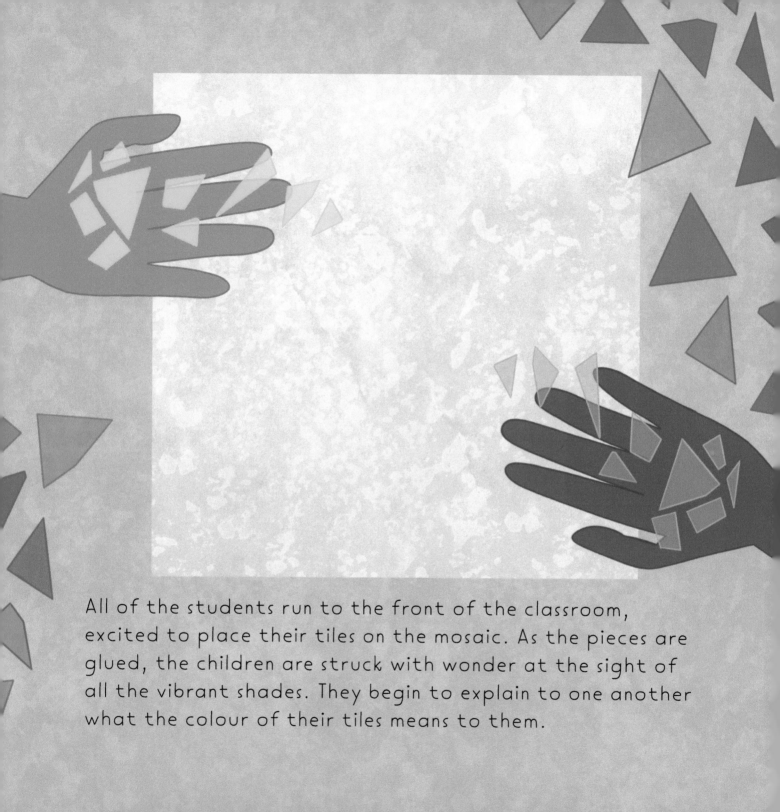

All of the students run to the front of the classroom, excited to place their tiles on the mosaic. As the pieces are glued, the children are struck with wonder at the sight of all the vibrant shades. They begin to explain to one another what the colour of their tiles means to them.

Beniko's tiles are the beautiful blush pink of the blissful cherry blossom trees that bloom on the grounds of Japan.

Mariano's tiles look like the magnificent orange sunset he marvels at while he eats his milky mango gelato in Italy.

Bridgette's tiles are the brilliant brown of the baguette in her hand and the beret on her head as she walks the breathtaking roads of France.

Louis' tiles remind him of his lucky catch on the light teal lake that he likes to fish on with his father as he connects to his Métis heritage in Canada.

Saniya's tiles are sunshine yellow like the stitching on her stylish sari from the sparkling streets of India.

Renshu's tiles are a radiant red, just like the racing rowboats used at the Dragon Boat Festival on the rivers of China.

Darina's tiles are a deep blue like the detailed dresses on her Ukrainian nesting dolls.

Tanashri's tiles are the purple of the tantalizingly tall coral reefs found in Tubbataha Reef National Marine Park, in the Philippines.

Talia takes a look at her golden tiles that match the towering pyramids on the tremendous sands of Egypt.

Pedro's tiles are a pearly white,
just like the pleasant sand
found on the peaceful shore of
Ipanema beach in Brazil.

Aleena's tiles are an amazing green that is seen on the age-old cedar trees that grow alongside her aunt's home in Lebanon.

Fabian's tiles are a fantastic blue, just like the fast-flowing water from the famous Dunn's River Falls in Jamaica.

Gabriella's tiles are the grey she sees while gazing at the great Mayan pyramids on the grounds of Mexico.

Carter's tiles are a cool crimson, just like the phone booth he calls friends from while sipping chamomile tea in the streets of England.

Isapoinhkyaki's tiles are indigo, just like the incredible sky behind an inuksuk built by an Inuit community in Northern Canada.

When their masterpiece is finished, the students step back to take in all the wonderful hues.

"You see, class," Miss Onya declares. "To make this image we needed to work as one, because Canada is a much brighter place when all the colours within it are appreciated."

Join Miss Onya's class as they discover that the beauty of Canada is found in the diversity of its people.

CPSIA information can be obtained
at www.ICGtesting.com
Printed in the USA
LVHW071728140222
710984LV00035B/953

9 781039 117761